For Clare and Kate - M.G.
For my mother - L.K.

Text copyright © Marilyn Malin 1993, 2014
Illustrations copyright © Lisa Kopper 1993, 2014

The moral rights of Margaret Graves and Lisa Kopper to be identified respectively as the
Author and Illustrator of this Work have been asserted by them in accordance
with the Copyright, Designs and Patents Act 1988.

First published in Great Britain under the title of *Stories from the Ballet* in 1993 by
Frances Lincoln Limited, 74-77 White Lion Street,
London N1 9PF

This edition first published in Great Britain and the USA in 2014

A CIP catalogue record for this book is available from the British Library

ISBN 978-1-84780-580-5

Printed in China

1 3 5 7 9 8 6 4 2

Ballet Stories

Margaret Greaves
Illustrated by Lisa Kopper

Contents

Giselle

Giselle was the prettiest girl in the village. She loved nothing so much as dancing. Sometimes her mother scolded her for it.

"You'll dance yourself into your grave, my girl, and become a sad ghost — a Wili."

The Wilis were said to haunt the depths of the forest. They were the spirits of girls betrayed by their lovers, who took their revenge by luring men to death with their dancing.

But Giselle only laughed.

"Have no fear, Mother. Loys and I will always love each other."

Loys had not long lived in the village, and nobody knew where he had come from, but already he had charmed Giselle's mother and all her friends. Sometimes Giselle tried to tease him into telling her more.

"You are unlike anyone else in the village. How can I be sure that you love me?"

Loys laughed. He picked a daisy and gave it to her.

"Ask the flower to tell you."

Giselle plucked the petals one by one, counting them as lovers have always done. "He loves me . . . he loves me not . . . he loves me . . ."

"He loves me!" cried Loys, plucking the last petal for her.

"See! The flower can't lie."

Giselle laughed with him and asked no more questions. It was enough that she trusted him.

Only Hilarion, the gamekeeper, disliked the newcomer. He had loved Giselle since they were both children and hoped to marry her. He was bitterly jealous of his rival and kept a close watch on him. One day he saw Loys speaking secretly to a youth whose manner was that of a royal squire. Hilarion was puzzled and suspicious. He waited for his chance to steal unobserved into Loys' cottage, and there he found what he had feared. A jewelled sword lay on the table with a princely mantle beside it. He caught up the sword and carried it away.

Outside there was laughter and singing as the village girls, led by Loys, went out to the vineyard to gather the grape harvest. Giselle stayed behind with her mother. But as the sound of her friends' voices died away, she was startled by another. A horn rang loud and clear from the forest, and out from the trees came a merry hunting party. She had never seen so splendid a company, for it was led by the Prince of Courland and his beautiful daughter Bathilde. Giselle gazed in excited admiration at their boots of fine embroidered leather, their gauntlets fringed with golden thread and their clothes of bright silk and velvet.

Her mother bustled out, curtseying a welcome.

"Don't just stand there, girl," she said to Giselle. "The lords and ladies are thirsty. Help me to serve them."

Together they set out wine and fruit for the unexpected guests. Princess Bathilde was enchanted with Giselle.

"Such prettiness and grace!" she exclaimed. "You must come back to court with me and be my own maid."

"Your Highness is kind," said Giselle shyly, "but I can never leave the village. I am soon to be married."

The princess smiled at her kindly.

"Then you must have a wedding gift."

She took off her golden necklace and clasped it round the girl's neck. Giselle curtsied her delighted thanks, then danced away to show the jewel to her friends, while her mother invited the royal party to rest in her cottage.

Soon afterwards Loys returned with the grape-gatherers, ready to celebrate the harvest. Giselle, chosen as queen of the festival, led them in a joyful dance. In her love and happiness she was swift and light and graceful as a flying bird.

But suddenly Hilarion was among them. White-faced and grim, he broke up the dance, parting the lovers with the jewelled sword which he thrust between them.

"Traitor! Deceiver!" he shouted. "Look at this blade! Look at the crest on the hilt! Albrecht, Duke of Silesia, you will never marry a peasant girl! You have stolen Giselle from me only to betray her. Let all the world know your treachery."

He lifted his horn and blew such a blast that even the prince and his daughter came out to see what was happening. Bathilde gave a startled cry.

"Albrecht! My betrothed! Why are you here, disguised in those peasant's clothes?"

Stricken with fear, Giselle looked from her lover to Princess Bathilde.

"No! No!" she whispered. "It is not true. Say it is not true! He is to marry me." She turned to face her lover. "Loys, why do you not deny it?"

The shame in his face and the anger in Bathilde's answered her only too clearly. With a cry of grief, Giselle snatched up the jewelled sword and plunged it into her own side.

Horror and pity held the watchers spellbound as Giselle began to dance. For a moment she moved as lightly as ever, as if in a dream of her lost happiness. Then she faltered, circling slowly, her eyes on Albrecht's face, weaker and weaker, until she fell like a dying bird into her mother's arms.

Heartbroken at the tragedy, all the village mourned their beloved Giselle. They buried her in a glade of the forest, beside a deep still

lake fringed with reeds and lilies.

One night, weeks later, Hilarion went to visit her grave. But as he entered the glade, thunder rolled out above him, will-o'-the-wisps flickered over the water and half-seen shapes moved stealthily between the trees. Hilarion drew back in fear, hiding himself in the bushes.

A woman's form rose glimmering from the lake, seeming to beckon. He knew her to be Myrtha, Queen of the dreadful Wilis. Other forms answered her call, gliding like swirls of mist out of the forest. Last of all she summoned Giselle herself from her grave to join their company.

Hilarion would have tried to escape, but someone else was approaching. Albrecht stepped out into the glade, bringing flowers for Giselle's tomb. He threw himself down upon it, weeping bitterly. Instantly Giselle was beside him.

"No, no! Your tears break my heart afresh. You are in dreadful danger here. Come quickly, let me hide you."

She drew Albrecht away, but as she did so, the other Wilis discovered Hilarion. In a moment he was surrounded by the pitiless dancers, white feet that circled him, white hands that drew him, nearer and nearer until too late he saw the black water at his feet, fell headlong, and was drowned within its depths.

"There is another man here," declared the queen. "Giselle, bring out your false lover."

"Hold fast to the cross on my grave," whispered Giselle. "It will protect you."

Then she cast herself at Myrtha's feet and pleaded for mercy.

"Dance!" commanded the queen. Her face was cold as winter frost. "Dance! Draw him to you."

Giselle was forced to obey. For a while Albrecht clung to the cross, resisting her unwilling spell. Then, overcome by longing, he forgot her warning, reaching out his arms. At once the Wilis closed in round him, pale and merciless, dancing, dancing, nearer and nearer the dark water. Only Giselle, braving their anger, tried to turn them back.

Suddenly a gleam of light touched the lake. A dawn wind rustled the trees. The night was passing, and with it the power of the Wilis was broken. The pale spirits dissolved into the morning light and Giselle sank back into her grave.

Albrecht reached out after her with empty hands, then fell weeping to the ground. Constant beyond death, Giselle had saved him from the vengeance of the Wilis.

The Firebird

Dusk was already falling in the forest and Prince Ivan was far from home. Menacing thunder rumbled overhead and he was anxious to find shelter from the gathering storm. He had nearly given up hope when he came unexpectedly to a high stone wall, above which the branches of orchard trees hung heavily, loaded with fruit. Bigger than the rest, its boughs arching high above theirs, was one that bore shining golden apples with a most enticing scent. Here perhaps was magic! But so much beauty seemed to promise goodness and hospitality. Ivan decided to risk climbing into the garden, for he could see no entrance.

Just then a flash of brilliant light swept the darkening sky and was gone. Ivan caught his breath in astonishment. The light had streamed from a bird, an exquisite creature with wings and tail like flame.

The light circled and came towards him once again. Swiftly Ivan fitted an arrow and took aim. Then in shame he lowered his bow as the bird passed overhead. Who could bear to harm so beautiful a creature?

Again the bird returned, flying low, and this time Ivan caught her in his hands. He held her fast, although she struggled desperately.

"Don't be afraid, dear bird," said Prince Ivan. "I mean you no harm. I will take you home with me. You shall have a golden cage,

the most delicate food, and servants to attend you. I will love you and make you happy."

The bird fluttered more wildly than before.

"Let me go," she begged. "I must be free. I should die in your golden cage."

Ivan's heart was touched with pity, although he could scarcely bear the thought of losing her. Reluctantly he opened his hands, but she did not at once fly free.

"Prince Ivan," she said, "you are wise and kind."

He felt no surprise that she knew his name, for the whole place smelled of magic. The bird bent her head and plucked a single shining feather from her wing, letting it fall at his feet.

"If danger ever threatens, hold up this feather and call for me. I will come."

Next moment she was gone, streaming golden fire like a comet. Ivan picked up the feather and thrust it inside his jacket. It seemed unlikely that a bird could ever help him, but he would always treasure this reminder of her beauty. Again the thunder rolled overhead, and he hurried to climb the wall and seek shelter in whatever house lay beyond it. The fruit trees were set in a garden of wide lawns and beds full of glowing flowers. There were tall iron gates in the wall on its further side, and just as his feet touched the grass they swung open. Ivan hid himself behind the nearest tree to watch.

Twelve young girls ran chattering into the garden, attending one who seemed to be their mistress. They circled the mysterious tree at the centre, plucking the golden fruit and tossing it to each other in play.

By now, dusk had given way to night, and by the rising moon Ivan saw the face of the one who looked like a princess. It was a sad and lovely face, gentle and kind. Ivan's heart went out to her. He left his hiding place and knelt at her feet.

"Lady," he begged her, "tell me who you are and where I am." The girl looked at him in wonder, but drew away as he tried to clasp her hands.

"Hush!" she whispered. "Whoever you are, speak low. There is danger here. This garden belongs to Kostchei the sorcerer. He will turn to stone anyone who trespasses on his ground."

"Then why are you here?" demanded the prince. "I am sure you are no sorceress."

The girl's eyes filled with tears that glittered in the moonlight.

"My maidens and I are his prisoners," she said. "We can never escape. Oh go! Go now, before he can find you."

"No," declared Ivan, grasping his dagger. "For your sake I defy him. I will rescue you from such evil power."

His last word was lost in the harsh clamour of a trumpet sounding beyond the wall. The girls fled to the iron gates like a flock of startled birds, and the princess called back over her shoulder.

"Run! Oh run! He is coming!"

A great peal of thunder rocked the sky. Ivan was plunged into sudden total darkness. Stumbling between the trees, he tried to find the iron gates, but when at last he reached them they were locked. As he shook at them in his despair, the iron bars melted away between his fingers. Light blazed round him as if from the glare of a thousand torches, and for a moment he thought he was in the hall of a great palace.

Then he realised that the columns were the trunks of tall trees, the fluttering tapestries were only leaves. A hideous face peered out at him, and then another. Slipping between the trees, dropping from the branches, crawling up from the ground, were scores of loathsome creatures. Black and twisted, demon-eyed and sharp-fanged, they danced all round him, shrieking and jeering, closing him in. There was no escape.

Once again the brazen trumpet sounded. Out from the forest strode the tall cloaked figure of Kostchei, the sorcerer. Behind him, weeping but helpless against the enchantment that drew them, followed the princess and her maidens.

"So you would steal my captives?" sneered Kostchei. "Do you think you can defy *me*? You enter my garden like a thief, but you shall stay there as a statue of stone."

The sorcerer raised dark arms like the wings of a huge bat and began to cast his spell. At that very moment Ivan felt the burst of the Firebird's feather against his skin. With sudden hope he snatched it out and held it high above his head, where it flickered like a living flame.

"Firebird! Firebird!" he called. "Come to my help."

With a rush of bright wings overhead, the Firebird flashed down to alight between him and his enemy. The evil torchlight paled and shrank in the radiance that flowed from her, like candles put out by the sun. Kostchei's threatening arms fell, the demon goblins cowered away.

"So!" said the Firebird. "Night horrors! Dark deformities! Have you come to dance at Prince Ivan's fate? Then dance you shall. Dance!"

Howling, yet forced to obey, under a magic more powerful than their master's, the wicked horde began to dance. Round and round, faster and faster, their lungs bursting, every limb in pain, the creatures whirled in a grotesque measure. They cried out for pity but the Firebird had no mercy, and one by one they collapsed and fell helpless to the ground. Only Kostchei still stood, rigid with fear and anger, as if he himself were made of stone.

"Prince Ivan," commanded the Firebird, "search among the roots of that hollow tree and bring out what you find there."

Kostchei shuddered, but the prince obeyed. From its hiding place at the bottom of the tree he drew out a golden casket encrusted with a thousand gems. At a sign from the Firebird he threw back the lid. Beneath it lay an enormous egg, pale and softly shining as an opal.

"Take it up," said the Firebird. "The sorcerer's wicked soul lives in that egg."

Kostchei rushed forward with a despairing cry.

"No! No! Give it to me! If it breaks, I shall die."

"Die then!" cried the prince.

He lifted the egg high and hurled it to the ground, where it broke like a splintered rainbow before utter darkness fell. Once again thunder rocked overhead, and through it pierced a terrible shriek of anguish. Silence followed. Then, slowly and gently as summer dawn, light flowed back. Prince Ivan stared about him.

The tree trunks were indeed the columns of a palace. He stood alone in a great hall lit by crystal lamps. Gone was the Firebird, gone were the demon goblins, gone was the sorcerer Kostchei. Music swelled and silver trumpets sounded as the doors of the hall swung open. Men and women in rich and stately procession flowed through them and greeted him with every sign of honour. Last of all, free and happy, came the princess and the twelve maidens of the once enchanted garden.

The prince and princess gazed at each other, silent in their joy. A shout went up from the courtiers.

"Prince, you have saved us. Stay and be our king. Long live our king and queen."

Quietly the two lovers met and clasped their hands together. Joy flowed from them, warm as the sun. Darkness and evil had vanished for ever, as a dream is dissolved by the day.

Ondine

The Lady Berta lived in a castle high above the sea. She was fond of her lover, Palemon, and intended one day to marry him, but she was capricious and wilful and often tormented him by pretending not to care for him at all.

One sunny autumn afternoon, Berta came back from hunting to find Palemon waiting for her at the entrance to her castle. He had come to offer her a precious amulet as a love token, but she was not in a mood to listen to him. She refused the jewel and swept past him into her castle, leaving him alone in the courtyard.

For a while Palemon waited. All was still, soundless except for the cool chiming fall of a small cascade in the garden. Its soft music caught his attention. A shadow moved behind the shining water and slim hands parted it as if it were a curtain. A water sprite darted out on to the rocks, silvery as a fish, then flitted down into the courtyard. Clearly she thought herself alone, for she was laughing and dancing for joy. Palemon moved quickly out of sight, afraid to disturb her. The sun was already low, casting a long shadow, and the nymph danced delightedly with the black shape, which seemed to imitate her every movement.

In her watery world there could be no shadows, and she was enchanted by this new playmate.

Palemon, watching, felt that he could never love anyone but this beautiful creature. Springing from his hiding place he tried to catch her in his arms. The startled sprite eluded his grasp like water, but still he pursued her until she paused to look at him.

"Loveliest of all spirits, who are you?" entreated Palemon. "Whence do you come?"

"I am Ondine. My home is in waves and waterfalls, for I am one of the nymphs of Tirrenio, Lord of the Sea." She glimpsed the amulet that hung round Palemon's neck and reached for it with curious fingers. "What is that thing you are wearing?"

Palemon unclasped the amulet for her to see.

"How pretty it is! It shines like the sun," cried Ondine.

With a quick movement she caught the golden chain out of his hand and danced away with it. Palemon tried to regain it, but she teased him, flitting always out of reach, until she tired of the game and tossed his treasure back to him. Next moment she had flashed away into the darkness of the forest and Palemon followed, calling to her to stay.

Ondine and Palemon had been so attracted by each other, caught up in their strange meeting, that they failed to see Berta come out of the castle. Angry and jealous, she summoned her hunting party and set out in pursuit of her faithless suitor.

Meanwhile, Palemon and Ondine had reached the sea shore where Tirrenio was watching his nymphs and strange sea creatures as they danced along the sands. He saw his favourite, Ondine, now hand in hand with a mortal lover, and swept fiercely between them.

"Away!" he cried to Palemon. "You have no right here. The man who loves a water sprite is in danger of his life."

He commanded his followers to drag the lovers apart, but they could not separate the pair. Before Tirrenio could prevent it, Ondine defiantly called for a hermit to marry her to Palemon. Then, loud and ominous, came the sound of a horn as Berta and her huntsmen appeared in close pursuit. They would have seized Palemon, had not the nymphs and sea creatures surged about them to terrify them into flight.

Then Palemon and his magical bride took ship so that they might live together in peace in some distant land. Neither knew that Berta, unaware of their marriage, was still following Palemon and had hidden herself aboard the same ship. She was watching one morning when Ondine was once again attracted by Palemon's amulet.

"Take it," said her husband, "I can deny you nothing."

Unable to endure her jealous pain, Berta ran between them.

"Faithless!" she cried to Palemon. "You are promised to me. The amulet is mine."

"Lady," said Palemon, pierced with remorse, "I have wronged you, but my love is given to Ondine. She is my wife."

"Take the amulet, and try to forgive us," begged Ondine, who could not bear to see Berta's distress.

Even as she spoke, a terrible figure rose from the sea. Tirrenio, as jealous of his favourite as Berta was of Palemon, had also been following the ship. He tore the amulet from Berta's hand.

"Wait! I will give you a better jewel," cried Ondine.

From the crest of a wave she caught up a necklace, a cascade of beads as frail-seeming and iridescent as bubbles, but strong as any precious stone. Berta shrank back.

"Witchcraft!" she accused her rival. "An accursed thing! Keep your gift." "Witchcraft?" echoed the watching sailors. They closed in, fearful and angry. "What is this creature? She is bringing a storm upon us."

Waves and winds were rising, battering the ship, stripping her sails, as Tirrenio attacked it in his fury. Out of the turmoil he arose and leaped on Ondine, carrying her away to the bottom of the sea. Berta and Palemon were swept away by the storm, but reached a rock where they clung for safety. A passing ship saw their distress and rescued them, and Berta took Palemon to her own castle.

Long weeks passed, until Berta's love and new tenderness made Ondine fade from Palemon's memory like a lovely but lost dream. In time he decided to marry Berta, knowing that she truly loved him. Berta's wedding day gift to her husband was a portrait of herself, and he happened to be gazing at it while she was greeting their guests. As Palemon looked at the portrait he saw there another face even more beautiful – the sad face of his true bride, Ondine, as she wept for him in her cave in the depths of the sea.

The wedding and the wedding guests seemed now unreal to Palemon. He cried Ondine's name aloud, and at once Tirrenio with his sea sprites swept in among the dancers. The frightened guests fled, taking Berta with them, while Ondine herself appeared to Palemon's longing eyes. With a cry of joy he ran to embrace her, but she escaped like a ghost out of his grasp.

"No, no! You must not kiss me. The touch of my lips would bring your death."

"Then I will die," declared Palemon, "for I can love no one but you."

Once again he caught her in his arms, bending his head to kiss her.

Mortal cannot marry immortal. As their lips touched, Palemon fell dying at Ondine's feet. Tirrenio swept the sea sprite away to the watery world where she belonged, but where no man could live. There in her cave she wept for many days, embracing her dead lover in her arms.

The Nutcracker

The Christmas tree stood tall and splendid by an uncurtained window, its candles glittering against the dark night sky outside. Clara and her brother Fritz watched the guests arriving for the party. More and more of them hurried in, with sparkling eyes and cheeks glowing from the cold, until the room was full of uncles and aunts and cousins and friends, old people and young ones, all ready to enjoy themselves.

Never was there such a party! They laughed and danced and played games until everyone was breathless.

Suddenly, from the shadows behind the Christmas tree a thin black figure stepped out into the room. The music wavered, the startled dancers drew back. Then they recognized Drosselmeyer, Clara's godfather, and laughed at their fright.

Clara loved her godfather, but he was so full of tricks and surprises that she sometimes wondered if he were really a magician! Tonight he had brought some puppets with him to amuse the company, and made them dance as if they were alive. Then he gave out his gifts, and these too were unexpected. Clara's brother received a hunting horn, but her own present was a nutcracker shaped like an ugly soldier doll.

Fritz snatched it from her.

"What a queer present! And he's hideous!"

"No, he isn't." Clara tried to snatch it back. "He just looks sad. And I love him."

Her naughty brother only laughed. He ran round the room, waving the nutcracker out of her reach. He was so rough and careless that in the end he broke it, and poor Clara burst into tears.

"Never mind!" Her godfather comforted her. "I can mend him for you."

He picked up the broken toy, and with skilful fingers had very soon repaired it.

All that evening Clara played with her ugly nutcracker soldier, and could not bear to leave him behind when she went to bed. At last, when the house was quiet, she crept downstairs and played with him until she fell asleep in front of the dying fire.

In a little while she began to dream.

It seemed that her godfather stood smiling down at her. The fire was burning brightly again, and the candles glowed on the Christmas tree, which seemed now as big as the biggest fir in the forest.

"Christmas Eve is a magical night, Clara," said Drosselmeyer. "Are you waiting for magic?"

Clara's heart jumped. She had been right – her godfather was not an ordinary person.

"Can you really work magic?" she whispered.

For answer, he lifted her into a big armchair, tucking her into the cushions to keep warm.

"Sit there safely and watch," he told her.

She heard whispers and laughter and the tapping of little feet. From the dark corners of the room all her favourite dolls came running.

She had collected dolls from everywhere – Chinese dolls and Indian dancers, dolls from Russia and England and Norway – and now they were all dancing together. Like the Christmas tree, they had mysteriously grown in size and were now as big as herself.

A sudden sound disturbed them, and they crowded together as if afraid. With a rustling and a scraping and a scurrying of grey furry bodies, out into the room marched a company of mice as big as the dolls. Their leader wore a crown and brandished a bright sword and frightened Clara with his glittering eyes and sharp white teeth.

They were met by a defiant trumpet call. Marching across the carpet to confront them was a regiment of her brother's toy soldiers, led by none other than her own ugly nutcracker.

The battle was fierce, and Clara watched in terror for her nutcracker's safety as he fought the Mouse King hand to hand. Suddenly she saw her favourite fall. Desperate to help him, she snatched off her slipper and threw it at his enemy with all her strength. Instantly the whole company of mice fled, but the nutcracker lay where he had fallen. Clara ran to him in tears and kissed him.

Then an astonishing thing happened.

At the touch of Clara's lips, the ugly nutcracker doll disappeared and a handsome young man sprang up in his place.

"Your gentleness has saved me!" he exclaimed. "How can I ever thank you?"

"She has broken half the spell," said Drosselmeyer, "but there is more to be done. Years ago the wicked Mouse Queen bit the Nutcracker Prince and transformed him into the doll I gave you. He could be changed to his own form again only by a girl who would love him despite his ugliness.

But he will not be wholly free until he has killed the terrible Mouse King."

Clara and the prince danced together in sheer delight at his return to his own shape, but Drosselmeyer soon broke in.

"Enough," he said. "You have no time to waste in finding the Mouse King. I am sending you both on a journey to a magic land. There, or on the way there, you will find him."

He lifted his gold-topped stick like a wand. The candles on the Christmas tree flickered and went out, leaving the room in darkness. Moonlight streamed in where the window had been, but now there was no window. Clara and the prince were standing outside beneath a huge fir tree laden with snow, with stars shining through its branches instead of candles.

"Oh look! Look!" whispered Clara.

The snowflakes falling all round them were turning into snow fairies, who swirled and danced like a cloud of soft white feathers. Then, mysteriously, the snowbound forest vanished, and Clara and her prince were gliding in a magic boat above a beautiful land of trees and flowers. There too were Clara's dolls, playing and dancing, until the menacing sound of a horde of pattering feet made them break off in fear and run to hide.

Sinister and threatening, the Mouse King and his army crossed the open glade, and melted into the shadows beyond it. The prince's sword flashed out.

"The time has come," he cried. "Now I will break the spell for ever."

Softly the ship came to earth and Clara and the prince descended. At this the dolls took courage, ran from their hiding places, and greeted them with joy. But their relief was all too short.

Grey shapes moved stealthily between the trees, long tails twirled, pointed teeth and twitching whiskers were all around them. At the Mouse King's signal the army broke cover and fell upon their enemy.

The prince fought so valiantly that very soon the mice were forced into retreat. Only the Mouse King held his ground. More and more desperate was his battle with the Nutcracker Prince until, to Clara's horror, they fell together into the dark underground passage that led to the Mouse King's home. Clara burst into tears, thinking she had lost her beloved prince for ever.

Now something was coming out from that dark entrance. She glimpsed the purple folds of the Mouse King's cloak and shrank in terror. But it was not the wicked mouse himself who reappeared, but the Nutcracker Prince, waving the trophy he had won.

"I am free!" he declared. "I have killed the Mouse King. The spell can never be repeated."

From every side, Clara's dolls ran out to greet him and celebrate his triumph. One after the other they delighted him with the beautiful dances of the countries from which they came.

Suddenly Drosselmeyer was among them, raising his long magician's hands as if to cast a spell.

The green wood faded, and once again Clara and the Nutcracker Prince were standing beneath the great snow-laden tree, its branches glittering with frost. Fairies flitted around it like shining butterflies, and the most beautiful of them all, dancing to delicate music, came to meet them.

"Welcome to the Land of Sweets!" she cried. "I am

its ruler, the Sugar Plum Fairy. We salute your victory."

At her summons, the other fairies gathered to honour her guests, and Clara and her prince danced together with them, radiant in their happiness. The fairies brought them royal robes, set silver crowns on their heads, and led them to seats of honour. Then once again they danced for their guests, in ever-changing patterns, circling and swirling like leaves in the wind. Clara's eyes began to dazzle as she watched them, the bright colours shimmered and merged, the music grew fainter . . . fainter . . . fainter . . .

Bewildered, Clara opened her eyes, to find herself curled on the hearth by the last embers of the fire. The Christmas tree stood dark against the window. Only her own bedroom candle burned where she had placed it on the table.

Her nutcracker doll had fallen from her hand, and she picked him up. She thought she had been dreaming about him, but she couldn't quite remember. Perhaps he *was* rather ugly, but she loved him just as he was. She smiled at him, holding him to her, while stars instead of candles glittered through the branches of the Christmas tree.

Swan Lake

It was the day before Prince Siegfried's twenty-first birthday. People flocked to the city to join in the celebrations, the feasting and dancing, for the young man was much loved. His mother, the queen, presented him with a splendid new crossbow, and he longed to try it out.

Only one thing dimmed his pleasure. Next day, for the sake of the kingdom, he must choose a bride. Six princesses, young, rich, and beautiful, had been invited to the ball, and one of these he must take. Though Siegfried knew his duty, he had never yet been in love and felt unready for marriage. He would rather go hunting than pay court to any princess.

Some of his friends sympathised with Siegfried's unhappiness.

"Sir," urged one of them, "why not enjoy this day while it is still yours? There is time enough left for you to go hunting."

"Indeed," agreed another. "Your Highness should try the queen's gift. And I have heard that strange white birds have been seen near the lake in the forest."

This was just the advice that the young prince wanted. He caught up his new crossbow and quickly formed a hunting party.

The hour was already late and it was nearly dusk when they drew near the lake. All talk and laughter stopped and they moved quietly forward.

Siegfried glimpsed white shapes moving between the trees.

"Wait here," he whispered. "So many of us would startle them. I will go on alone."

Slowly and cautiously he crept forward, slipping from tree to tree. Now he saw that the great white birds were swans. Some were already floating on the smooth water, others flying down to join them. The prince marked one of these, knelt, and raised his bow to shoot.

His hand was already on the string when, just as his chosen swan touched the ground, an amazing thing happened. The bird's head drooped, the strong white wings folded, the feathers fell away, and from their shining softness stepped a girl more lovely than Siegfried had ever imagined. All round her the other swans too, as they alighted or swam to the shore, where changed. They shed their glimmering feathers and rose up from them as graceful young girls. Marvellous as they were, the prince had eyes only for the girl he had first seen.

With beating heart he ran forward to speak to her, but his movement was too sudden. Frightened as if she were truly a bird, she shrank from his outstretched hands. The prince followed her through the gathering shadows, calling softly to reassure her. In a tree high above them an owl hooted, a harsh menacing sound, and the girl ran from him.

Siegfried dropped his crossbow and knelt in the grass until at last she ceased to elude him, and waited timidly for him to speak.

"Lady," said the prince, "you are in no danger from me. How could I ever harm someone so beautiful? Only, I beg you, explain this mystery."

The girl looked at him and saw that he was kind and gentle, and knew that she could trust him.

"I am the Princess Odette," she said. "Alas for me, I rejected the wicked sorcerer Rothbart, and in revenge he turned me and my maidens into the swans you have just seen. At night we regain our human form, but at the first touch of dawn-light we become swans again."

Siegfried was horrified.

"Is there no hope? No power that can break the spell?"

Again an owl hooted in the gathering darkness.

"Hush!" whispered Odette. "Speak softly so that Rothbart cannot hear. For he watches us all night in the form of an owl."

Even a brave man may feel a prickle of fear, so near to an unseen powerful magician, but the prince hardened his courage.

"Tell me," he urged her again. "Is there no way?"

"Yes," murmured Odette. "There is one. If someone who has never loved before could love me faithfully and keep his vow, the spell could be broken."

Siegfried took her hands in his with a cry of joy.

"Then you shall be free, Odette. For you are my first and only love, and I swear that I will be faithful as long as I live."

Rashly he had spoken aloud. As he drew the princess towards him there was a rush of great wings overhead. With glaring eyes and fierce spread talons, a huge owl swept between them, hurling them apart. Siegfried snatched up his crossbow and took aim as the hideous bird circled above them, but Odette threw herself in the way.

"No! No!" she shrieked in terror. "His life and mine are bound together by the spell. At the very moment that one of us dies the other will die too."

At that the prince dropped his bow and tried to stand between her and her tormentor. But once again the owl swooped over them, dragging Odette back with his claws and blinding them both with his beating wings.

"Go! Go!" cried Odette. "For my sake, go. Be faithful, be true. Remember your vow."

There was sudden silence and stillness. The owl had gone, and only a group of snow-white swans sailed on the darkened waters of the lake.

The prince could do nothing but return to the palace, filled with grief and anger, but determined that by love and courage he would at last defeat the magician. He went through the next day in a dream, and in a dream took part in the ball given in his honour. He danced with each of the six princesses and was courteous to them all, but told his mother that he could marry none of them. The queen was in despair.

Suddenly a fanfare of trumpets rang out above the music, the ballroom doors swung wide, and heralds ushered in a magnificent personage with his daughter on his arm.

The Master of Ceremonies announced, "The Knight of the Black Swan and Her Excellency his daughter."

With a cry of joy Siegfried hurried forward to greet the new guests. The knight's daughter in her black velvet gown and her

glittering coronet of diamonds had the face of his beloved Odette. He was so enthralled by her beauty that he never looked closely at her father. Handsome and dignified though he was, the knight's mouth was cruel and there was a dangerous mocking glitter in his eyes. He was the dreaded sorcerer Rothbart who, by his evil arts, had caused his own daughter Odile to look exactly like the Princess Odette.

Siegfried took her hand and led her into the dance, his face alight with happiness. Odile moved with him as gracefully as a swan, her eyes seeming full of love. Close to them always hovered the enchanter, weaving a spell to bind them together.

There was a desperate knocking at one of the windows of the hall but, spellbound by Rothbart's upraised hand, no-one saw or heard the white wings beating wildly against the glass. As the dance ended, Rothbart stepped forward and joined the hands of Siegfried and Odile together. "Prince," he said, "I see how greatly my daughter is honoured by your admiration. She shall be yours if you will swear before this company that you will love her and no other for ever."

Siegfried gazed, entranced, at the face of the false Odette. "I swear," he said. "This lady and none other shall be my bride."

At the same moment he was horrified to see the looks of his partner change.

Petrushka

"Hurrah! The fair is coming! Hurrah! Hurrah!"
Little boys shouted the news through the snow-drifted streets of St Petersburg and everyone hurried out to the market square. The fair was a great event in the year, cheering the long cold winter. There would be sideshows and roundabouts, acrobats and conjurers, stalls selling sweetmeats and laces and ribbons. Best of all, there would be a puppet show.

Sure enough, as the carts and wagons rolled in, the puppet-master set up his booth.

"Walk up! Walk up!" he shouted. "See my living puppets. Watch them dance for you. Come, ballerina!"

Out from the booth danced the most beautiful doll, moving as if she were really alive. The crowd gasped. They were delighted, yet half-afraid. But though they thought the puppet-master was clever, no one guessed the truth. He was really a wicked and heartless magician. He had given life to his puppets but cared for them not at all. He wanted only the money that they made for him.

All round the square flitted the ballerina, smiling and vain, her golden hair shining in the light of the street lanterns.

She too cared for no one but herself, but was sure that everyone loved her.

"Petrushka!" called the magician.

The shy, awkward figure of Petrushka the clown sidled out of the booth. He was an old puppet and his clothes were by now rather shabby. He adored the ballerina and wanted to dance with her, but she laughed at him and twirled out of his reach. Everyone clapped, thinking it a great joke.

"Soldier!" commanded the magician.

A Moorish soldier, dark-skinned and handsome, wearing a splendid uniform, stalked out into the square. The ballerina ran to join him. The soldier was as vain and selfish as she was. He liked the beautiful doll to flirt with him and was very jealous if she looked at anyone else, but there was no real love in his cold heart.

"Enough!" called the showman after a while.

At once the puppets collapsed on the ground, lifeless things made only of cloth and straw. Their owner threw them into their boxes, kicking Petrushka carelessly as he did so.

In their boxes, out of sight of the crowd, the dolls became alive again. Tired and aching and unhappy, the poor clown tried to climb out and escape, but his master saw him and threw him back. Petrushka tried to cheer himself by thoughts of his beloved ballerina. He was too humble to expect her to love him in return, but he hoped that she might at least give him a kind look or word.

Suddenly he heard light footsteps and there beside him was the ballerina herself. She smiled at him carelessly, and Petrushka was almost speechless with joy.

"I'm dreadfully bored all by myself," she complained. "Amuse me, Petrushka."

Petrushka jumped up, delighted to play his clown's part for her. He was ready to be as ridiculous as she liked if only it would please her. The ballerina laughed at his antics. Then he grew bolder and tried to stammer out his love, but at that the foolish doll took fright and ran away. He called after her but she wouldn't listen.

"It was my fault," he reproached himself. "I was too rough and sudden for someone so finely bred, so delicate. My clumsiness has frightened her away."

Then Petrushka remembered the ballerina's laughter and took heart.

"I believe she does like me a little," he said. "I will find her and be very gentle then perhaps she will stay."

The wicked showman had gone off into the town, so the puppets were free for a while to do what they liked. Filled with new hope, Petrushka went in search of his beautiful lady.

Meanwhile the ballerina had recovered from her fright, but she was still bored. She sought out the Moorish soldier, expecting him to flatter and admire her. But the soldier was far too busy admiring himself! He was gazing into a mirror, twirling his moustaches and trying out different attitudes. He took no notice at all of the ballerina.

Her vanity was hurt. Determined to have his attention, the ballerina tossed her golden hair, shook out her skirt, and pirouetted and danced and smiled until at last the soldier was forced to notice her.

He caught her in his arms, and they laughed and flirted, so engrossed with each other that they never noticed the arrival of Petrushka.

Poor sad clown! He had come in such hope and happiness, only to find his beloved ballerina in the arms of his rival. But his distress was even more for her than for himself, for he knew that the soldier was fierce and jealous.

"Oh no, no!" he cried. "Don't trust him, ballerina. He will be cruel and faithless."

The dancers whirled round to look at him.

"Petrushka, you stupid clown!" stormed the doll, her pretty face sharp and ice-edged with rage. "How dare you follow me? Go away."

"I only want to protect you," pleaded Petrushka.

At that, the soldier ran across the room and knocked him down.

"Protect her?" he jeered. "You miserable, scrawny thing! Who are you to protect her? You insult me. Off with you! Out!"

As the clown scrambled up, the soldier kicked him and chased him out with blows from the flat of his sword.

Outside in the square a crowd was waiting for the return of the puppet-master and the next show. They were startled to hear thuds, shouts, and cries from inside the booth. Suddenly Petrushka darted out between them, shaking and white with terror. Behind him skipped the ballerina, shrieking abuse.

"Stupid, ugly thing! How dare you say you love me? I never want to see you again."

Out of the booth behind her rushed the soldier. He pushed the ballerina aside, pursuing the clown with his upraised scimitar.

"Out of the way!" he roared to the crowd. "Run, Petrushka, run!

I'll punish you for your impudence."

Petrushka ran. He stumbled through the snowdrifts, gasping for breath, running now for his life. But the soldier was younger and stronger and cruel. The clown tripped and fell. His enemy leaped upon him. The edge of his wicked shining scimitar struck down on Petrushka's neck, and the clown's body crumpled to the ground.

Just then the magician himself returned, and the ballerina and the soldier slipped back into the booth. The showman pushed through the clamouring crowd, some of them frightened, some of them weeping for pity. Bending over Petrushka, he laughed and picked him up, dangling the limp form by its head.

"What a fuss about nothing!" he mocked. "Did you really think this scarecrow was alive? It was my magic that moved him. Look, it's only a ragged straw puppet."

He shook the sad little bundle so that sawdust, not blood, trickled from the wound. The crowd muttered, but began to move away. The showman set off for his lodging, jingling the money he had taken that day, looking forward to his supper and a good fire. With one hand he trailed Petrushka's body through the snow.

"He was always a poor thing," he said to himself. "I was tired of him and I'm glad he's broken. I'll make a new puppet, more handsome than the Moorish soldier and a better dancer than the ballerina."

His thoughts broke off, interrupted by a great cry behind him, and his cruel careless heart turned to ice as he looked back. Above the puppet booth, shining in the moonlight, loomed the figure of Petrushka — no longer the pitiful clown, but a terrible avenging phantom!

The wicked showman fled in terror from those accusing eyes, leaving the broken puppet on the ground. But Petrushka's spirit was free, free from his bondage to the magician, free from his love for the worthless ballerina and his fear of the soldier, free to be himself at last.

The Sleeping Beauty

There was a tremendous bustle at the court of King Florestan and his queen. Their first child, the infant Princess Aurora, was to be christened.

"Are you *sure* we've invited everyone who matters?" asked the king for the fourth time.

"Of course, dear," his wife soothed him. "You gave the list to the Lord Chamberlain yourself."

Still not satisfied, the king summoned the Lord Chamberlain.

"But of course, sire!" said the Lord Chamberlain. "I gave the list to my secretary, who sent out all the invitations." He summoned his secretary to give him the list, which he handed with a flourish to the king.

"Hmm. All the nobles, I see. And some less important people too — that always makes a good impression. Give a special welcome to the child's godmothers, the Lilac Fairy and her five sisters. We have great expectations of their christening gifts."

Just then a flourish of trumpets announced the arrival of the guests, first the nobility, then the commoners, followed by the six fairy godmothers and a whole train of other fairies.

The king looked slightly worried.

"Did we invite *all* these?" he whispered.

"Hush, dear!" murmured the Queen. "You know how they like to go about in bands."

The fairies surrounded the cradle and announced their gifts to the Princess Aurora. The five younger fairy sisters spoke first and endowed the child with health, grace, beauty, good humour and riches. But just as the Lilac Fairy was about to speak, the torches flickered in a cold wind, the hall darkened as if in a thunderstorm, and harsh and dreadful sounds were heard at the door.

The queen turned pale. The king shouted to the guards, but they fell back helpless before the hideous horde that streamed into the hall – owl-faced, bat-winged, cat-tailed – drawing a dragon throne on which sat a black-robed ancient fairy.

"Carabosse!" gasped King Florestan in horror.

Everyone in the kingdom had heard that dreaded name, but no one had seen her for fifty years or more, and it was supposed that she had died or gone away.

The aged creature descended, gazing round with proud and angry eyes.

"Ha, a feast, I see! Every fairy in the land invited. Except me!"

"Madam," said the queen hurriedly, "you are most welcome. Surely the invitation was sent out? We have been most particular, as you say, to invite *every* fairy in the land."

"*Every* fairy!" declared the king. "I told the Lord Chamberlain so myself."

"*Every* fairy!" agreed the Lord Chamberlain. "I told my secretary so myself."

"*Every* fairy!" echoed the secretary. He knew the mistake would be blamed on him. It always was.

But Carabosse was not satisfied. Dark with anger, she raised her wand over the baby's cradle.

"When the princess is sixteen," she shrieked, "she shall prick her finger on a spindle, and die."

In the horrified gasp that followed, the Lilac Fairy stepped forward.

"I have not yet made my gift," she said. "I cannot wholly defeat this evil magic, but the Princess Aurora shall not die. She shall sleep for a hundred years, when the spell will be broken by the first prince who kisses her."

Carabosse spat at her like a furious cat, but now the other fairies closed in. Step by step they drove her back, and her ugly servants dragged her off into the darkness.

The queen was deeply grateful for the Lilac Fairy's help, though she did worry about the unknown prince.

"Princes aren't always what they used to be," she confided to her husband. "Who knows what sort of man the dear child may have to marry!"

"We may yet prevent it," said the king.

Determined to outwit the wicked fairy, he at once outlawed the use of spindles, or even knitting needles, upon pain of death. Woollen dresses and shawls went completely out of fashion. The little princess was quite unaware of the trouble she was causing, and unconscious of any danger. She grew in grace and beauty and all other gifts until her sixteenth birthday.

The festivities on this great occasion were almost marred by the discovery of a group of young women who had not heard the king's decree, and who were arrested with knitting in their hands. Only the intercession of the queen saved them from execution. She would not let anything spoil the celebration to be held in the palace, when the Princess Aurora was to choose a husband from one of the four princes who courted her. Aurora flirted and danced delightfully with all of them, light as a flower in the wind, but none of them touched her heart.

Towards midnight, an old countrywoman entered the hall, begging leave to greet the princess with a posy of flowers from her garden.

Delighted with the flowers and wishing to be kind to one of her father's humblest subjects, Aurora took the posy and began to dance with it. A minute passed, then the princess gave a little cry as something like a thorn pricked her finger. The flowers

fell from her hand, and with them the spindle which had been cunningly hidden among them. There was a shriek of mocking laughter as the Fairy Carabosse threw off her peasant disguise and fled from the hall. With a yawn and a sign, Aurora fell at her parents' feet, fast asleep.

"My poor child," wept the queen. "If she wakes after a hundred years she will find herself alone."

"Have no fear," said the Lilac Fairy. "Take her up and lay her on her bed."

Sorrowfully the attendants obeyed her. As the royal parents followed to their daughter's room, the Lilac Fairy called all her sisters. Unseen by anyone, they ran all about the palace, and whoever or whatever they touched fell into a sleep as deep as Aurora's. The cooks snored in the kitchen, the guards slept in the doorways, the guests fell dreaming just where they had danced, the cats curled on the cushions and dogs lay under the table.

Then the Lilac Fairy cast a spell all round the palace itself. A vast wood instantly grew up round it, and dense thickets of bramble crowded between the trees until no one could have guessed what lay within.

Exactly one hundred years later, a young prince was out hunting. Wishing to be alone for a while, he dismissed his attendants and wandered alone on the edge of this dark forest. It seemed a strange and eerie place and very silent. No birds sang there, no small creatures disturbed the undergrowth.

Suddenly a voice startled him.

"Welcome, Prince Florimund!"

The young man's sword flashed out on guard until he saw, amazed, that a whole company of fairies barred his way. Their leader was smiling at him.

"Who – who are you?" stammered the prince.

"I am the Lilac Fairy. Your Highness has been long expected. The Princess Aurora awaits your coming. See!"

As the fairy spoke, a girl of amazing beauty glided from between the forest trees. The prince moved towards her, enchanted, and danced with her as if in a dream until she slipped away from him into the forest.

"It was only a vision," said the Lilac Fairy. "The real Princess Aurora is held captive by a spell, in a castle deep in the forest. Only you can save her. Follow. I will show you the way." Instantly Prince Florimund plunged after her between the trees. Roots tripped him, brambles tore him, branches bruised him, but he forced his way through doggedly, slashing down every obstacle. Then noises began, shrill whistles, shrieks and ugly laughter. An ancient black crone of a fairy stood in his path, attended by demon-faced, bat-winged creatures with glaring eyes. Nothing daunted, the prince laid about him with his sword till the whole horde fled screaming into the darkness. Next moment he had emerged from the wood and stared about him in astonishment.

Night had fallen, but in the moonlight he saw that he was standing in a garden where roses rioted everywhere amidst grass as high as his waist. In front of him reared an old grey palace, its doors standing wide open. Cobwebs draped the outside of every window and hung in grey curtains across the doorway where six men-at-arms lay asleep. His sword ready in his hand, the prince stepped over them. He entered a hall where richly dressed men and women lay fast asleep on the floor. Their clothes were in his great-grandparents' fashion and covered with dust. There were no cobwebs to be seen, for all the spiders were asleep.

Prince Florimund crossed the hall and climbed the main staircase. Chambermaids were sleeping beside half-made beds, footmen lay unconscious in the corridors. At the very end of a long passage, he entered a room with curtains of silk and hangings of damask and a golden bed on a raised dais. In a chair on either side of it slept a king and queen, both with their crowns awry. The bed coverlet was faded, but not the girl who lay upon it, the princess whom he had seen in his vision in the wood.

He called her name loudly, but still she slept on. So he bent and kissed her. The princess opened her eyes, looked at her rescuer, and instantly fell in love. As soon as she sat up, the king and queen woke too, the lords and ladies in the hall, the guards and cooks and maids, the dogs and cats and spiders and the mice in the attics. Chatter and laughter filled all the rooms.

Aurora's parents were delighted to find their daughter in love with such an eligible prince.

"When you think whom it might have been!" the queen sighed in relief.

They agreed that the young couple should be married immediately — that is, as soon as possible after the palace had been dusted, the queen had learned the latest fashions, and the Lilac Fairy had removed the enchanted forest.

A great ball was held to celebrate the royal wedding, attended by friends already famous in story — the Bluebird and his mate, Puss-in-Boots and the White Cat, Red Riding Hood and the Wolf — and, of course, by the Lilac Fairy and all her sisters. Carabosse alone was not invited, for she had fled the kingdom and was never seen again.

Coppelia

There was once an old magician called Dr Coppelius. He lived in a tall old house in a quiet old town, where he was famous for the wonderful clockwork toys that he made.

At last he created a life-size doll so beautiful that he fell in love with her. He gave the doll a name very like his own – Coppelia.

"I'm sure," he crowed, "that when people see her they will think she is really alive. She will trick them all. I'll prove it."

He set her carefully in a chair by the window of his upstairs workroom, so that she seemed to be looking down into the street. Then, chuckling at his joke, the old magician kept out of sight, and watched.

Soon young Swanilde passed that way, humming to herself as she thought of her lover Franz, and feeling friendly to all the world. Glancing up, she caught sight of Coppelia.

"Good morning," she called cheerfully. "Are you visiting Dr Coppelius?"

Getting no answering smile, she tried again.

"Don't be shy! I'm sure we can be friends."

The strange girl only stared at her blankly, without a word.

"What a rude girl!" said Swanilde, offended. "Well, if you want to be so proud, I'm sure I don't care."

She flounced off, not knowing that her lover was following a little distance behind her. As Franz passed the magician's house, he too looked up. He was pleased and interested to see such a pretty girl.

"You shouldn't be up there all alone," he called to her. "Come down, and let us talk."

The beautiful girl took no notice of him. But, unluckily for Franz, Swanilde heard his voice, turned her head, and ran back. Then she saw that he was talking to Coppelia.

"How dare you flirt with that horrid girl?" she demanded, boxing his ears angrily as she pulled him away down the street.

In his hiding place Dr Coppelius laughed and hugged himself. His darling Coppelia could make anyone mistake her for a living girl.

That day it was announced that the lord of the manor had given a new church bell to the town. To celebrate the event, he would give a bag of gold to all the couples who were to be married that month. Franz and Swanilde, who had quickly made up their quarrel, were delighted. But each of them was still secretly very curious about Dr Coppelius' beautiful visitor.

In the evening the old magician went out for a stroll, planning how to deceive more people, and wishing that his wonderful doll were really alive so that he could marry her. Lost in thought, he was so startled when some naughty boys jumped out at him that he dropped his keys, and never missed them.

A few minutes later the keys were found by Swanilde, who was walking with some of her friends.

"Now's our chance," she cried delightedly, "while Dr Coppelius is out. Let's go in and find that strange girl!"

Laughing and full of curiosity, the girls trooped in and climbed the stairs to the workroom, leaving the door unlocked behind them. Coppelia still sat in the window.

"Now," said Swanilde, "you will surely talk to us. There's no need to be so shy. We all want to be friends."

She lifted Coppelia's hand, and was startled to find it hard, cold, and unresponsive. Alarmed, she bent her head and listened anxiously for a heart beat. Then she looked into the blank blue eyes, and laughed.

"Why, she's only a doll! Dr Coppelius is playing a trick on us all. Madam, shall we dance?"

She picked up Coppelia and swung her round, pretending to waltz with her.

"What a strange room this is," said one of her friends, "full of dolls as big as we are, that look almost alive! Look at this Chinaman!"

The Chinese doll toppled and fell as she touched it. With a startled jangling sound its limbs began to jerk into life, and the intruders jumped back, scared. Then they realised that they had accidentally started the doll's mechanism.

"Let's make them all work, and then dance with them," cried another girl.

Laughing, they ran about the room, starting up all the other dolls – a man playing a guitar, a soldier in a smart uniform, another dressed like a Persian Prince. Round the room they whirled, having such fun that they never heard the magician's foot on the stair. The old man burst in, furious, shouting that they had ruined all his work.

Three of the frightened girls fled, past him and out of the house, but Swanilde was too late. Then she had a clever idea. While Dr Coppelius chased her friends she quickly changed her dress with the doll's and hid Coppelia in a cupboard. When the doctor came panting back he found the false Coppelia sitting in the chair by the window, apparently just the same as before. She stared ahead unblinking, her arms and legs as stiff as wood.

Swanilde was afraid in case Dr Coppelius looked too closely, but just then there was a scraping noise at the window, the top of a ladder appeared, and then the head of her lover Franz. He too was looking for Coppelia.

Franz was very startled to discover that the old man had already come home, and was even more surprised that Dr Coppelius actually opened the window for him, and invited him in. Little did he know that the magician was inwardly raging that his beloved doll had been laughed at, and that he was planning a dreadful revenge.

"Come in, my young friend, do come in," said Dr Coppelius. "You must have a glass of wine with me, and then you shall see *all* my dolls."

He offered a glass of rich dark wine that sparkled in the light. Franz drank it cheerfully, unaware of the magic potion so artfully mixed with it. Almost instantly he was sound asleep, and the old man chuckled as he reached for his book of spells.

"Now I will get my own back on you all. Sleep on, young man, while I draw your soul from your body and give it to my Coppelia. You will sleep for ever, but *she* will live. I shall have the most beautiful wife in the world!"

Swanilde heard him, and smiled secretly as she made her own plan. Very soon Dr Coppelius bent over her, muttering a strange incantation. Very slowly, she began to move. She turned her eyes, and then her head. She lifted a straight stiff arm and then a leg.

"It works! The spell works!" cried Dr Coppelius, lifting her from her chair.

Holding her stiff hand, he urged her to walk, and she moved forward with short jerky steps, like a mechanical toy. Then she began to walk more freely, more and more like an ordinary girl.

"My darling Coppelia!" cried the enraptured magician.

He tried to kiss her but she whisked out of reach and began to tease him, dancing away with the other dolls, until she suddenly snatched the sword from the clockwork soldier and chased the old man all round the room.

There was a sudden noise of clapping and laughter in the doorway. Swanilde's friends had plucked up courage to come back for her, and were amazed at what they saw. They thought it a huge joke. Now Dr Coppelius realised that he in his turn had been tricked, and he screamed so loudly with rage that Franz woke up from his enchanted sleep. Swanilde caught him by the hand, and all the young people escaped out of the house.

Next day a great celebration was given by the lord of the manor, who kept his promise to endow all the engaged couples with a bag of gold. But just as the merriment was at its height, there was a sudden uproar. Dr Coppelius rushed forward, shouting for justice.

"They have broken my dolls," he declared, "and I shall have to repair every one. They have mocked me and my beautiful Coppelia. I have been shamefully treated!"

He was so outraged that Franz and Swanilde felt rather ashamed of their pranks.

"It is true," admitted Swanilde, "though we did it only for fun. We never meant to harm anything. Dr Coppelius, please forgive us. We will give you our bag of gold to show how sorry we are."

"No," said the lord of the manor. "Keep your gift. I will have no one unhappy on this happy day. I will give a bag of gold to Dr Coppelius also."

Everyone cheered, and Franz and Swanilde drew the old magician into a dance until at last he laughed with them. Next day he repaired Coppelia, and brought her out for all the town to see. Everyone said that she was the most wonderful doll ever made, and that there was no one in the world as clever as their Dr Coppelius. As for the old magician, he never again tried to make a living doll.